Happy Buthday
1982

love from gran'ma

D1400483

Duey's Tale

OTHER BOOKS BY PEARL BAILEY

The Raw Pearl
Talking to Myself
Pearl's Kitchen

DUEY'S TALE
Pearl Bailey

HARCOURT BRACE JOVANOVICH
New York and London

COPYRIGHT © 1975 BY PEARL BAILEY

All rights reserved. No part of this publication
may be reproduced or transmitted in any form or
by any means, electronic or mechanical, including
photocopy, recording, or any information storage
and retrieval system, without permission in
writing from the publisher.

Printed in the United States of America

PHOTOGRAPHS BY ARNOLD SKOLNICK AND GARY AZON

DESIGNED BY ARNOLD SKOLNICK

Library of Congress Cataloging in Publication Data

Bailey, Pearl.
    Duey's tale.

    SUMMARY: A maple seedling becomes separated from
his mother tree, makes friends with a bottle and a log,
and searches for his own place in life.
    [1. Seeds—Fiction. 2. Trees—Fiction] I. Title.
PZ7.B1528Du   [Fic]   74-22278
ISBN 0-15-126576-3

First edition

B C D E

Duey's Tale

The winds howled, but the tree stood fast, determined to hold on to what was hers. This year's bounty of baby seeds was her largest. She was proud. And why not? Motherhood is the greatest joy that can happen. Blow, wind! Her nursery was safe, her boughs strong. The wind slowed as the night ended. Now to wake her babies. They were already stirring in her leafy skirt.

She stood tall and silent. Was not life beautiful? Her arms caught the noon sun's brilliance and held it briefly, then flung it through her lacy leaves in a splash of gold.

3

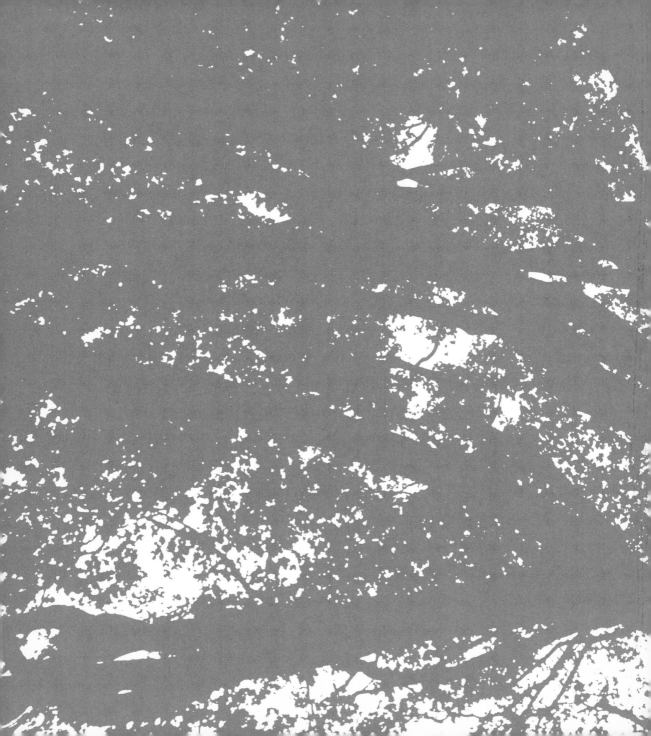

School buses unloaded boys and girls by the dozens and they stood before her, heads thrown back, tiny mouths open. Such was fame. "Look, my children," she called to her seedlings, "look at the boys and girls. Now, don't shake and rustle around like that," she cautioned them. "Where are your manners?"

"But Mama, we're not shaking for fun! It's the wind, Mama, that's shaking US." The seedlings fluttered, each one with his leafy wings twisting in the air like little propellers.

Oops—there was the wind again, a big blast. Folding her arms quickly to protect her brood, she began to count her babes. Let's see, she mused, 1, 2, 20, 29—oh no! It's not possible! 1, 2, 20, 29—oh! Dear Lord, oh dear Lord— a child is missing. It's the youngest, Duey,

Wait—over there—what is that boy twirling in his hand? It's, it's . . . horror of horrors . . . it's Duey. She screamed, "Bring back my child, put him down, bring him back." Then, in the language of the forest, she pleaded, but no one heeded her. The boys and girls trooped back to their buses.

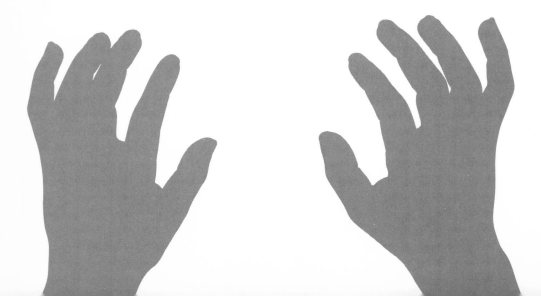

Another gust. She knew, sooner or later, that all her seedlings would fly off, but it wasn't time yet. The wind was supposed to lift off their little propellers, but not yet, not yet. "Mama! Mama!" She heard the pitiful cry. She could see the tiny fellow scrambling against the wind, then she heard a last cry, "Mama" — and he was gone. Dear God, watch over Duey.

Duey sat on the grass and cried. Where to go? What to do? He tried to remember what Mama had to say about feeling sorry for one's self. Somehow, he couldn't remember. He gulped. "Now I remember!" said Duey to himself. "Mama said not to fret, but instead to go on to the next thing." Next things next, then, Duey. Go the way of the wind.

Spinning lightly through the grass, he suddenly came upon something unbelievable to the eye. It was a large glassy-looking thing, neither grass nor earth. He went to the edge, as far as he dared, and took a peep. "Someone's looking at me," he cried. It had startled eyes in a round face like his own, and two green sprouting wings.

"Why, it's me," said Duey. Duey was proud to have figured this out by himself—and that was his first mistake. Too much pride is not a nice thing, not even in beginners. Duey was fascinated by his image. Out came his tongue: out came the image's. How funny! Back and forth he rocked, gaining and losing the image. First you see me, then you don't. The more he rocked, the harder he laughed. So much fun, and he did not even have to share it with anyone. Back farther— over farther— and *oops*— tipping— hold on—H-E-L-P.

Duey was on his back, floating down the river. But he wasn't wet! He was riding along on something that felt rough and hard. Suddenly a voice called, but from where? The river? The sky?

"Gabby's the name." The voice sounded loud and snappy. "I'm a log, a fairly big log, you know. I'm on my way downstream, just lazing along. No hurry, cause life's a drag, man—a big nothing. What I'm doing, man, is splitting the scene. My folks put me down. Everybody's in my way, calling me weird. Man, they just don't dig. So I'm losing those cats, cause they can't communicate. Yes, sir! I'm just flooaating along."

"Gee, Gabby, you don't give the world much of a break, do you?" Duey asked. But he asked in a soft tone; he wanted to make friends with this fellow.

"You punk," said Gabby. "You're no different from everybody else, a big drag. So flake off." And with that, Gabby started tossing himself from side to side, rolling fast.

Duey was terrified. Suppose Gabby held him under the water? Gabby was a large fellow, but then, size does not make the man. "Son, do not run from life, but calmly walk away from strife," Mama had often said. Well, Mama, Duey thought to himself, here I go, and without another thought, he jumped off the raging Gabby's back. Gabby rollicked with laughter.

Ahead of him Duey saw scads of wiggly things, large and small, green and blue with pink faces, scads and scads of wigglies. He ducked and bobbed, but the fish swam right by him. Then something was sucking him in—in, but not under. ZIP—he was trapped inside a strange object that was fat in the stomach and skinny at the end. Which end was which? He could see water; in fact, he was in water, but not deep enough to float. All around him everything was clear as glass. Glass? That's it! He was inside a bottle.

A bottle? "Yes," the bottle said, "I'm Slicker. Take it easy and you won't drown." She spoke softly, and right off Duey could tell that Slicker had a lot of warm good feeling, like Mama. "Sit tall, and you won't drown. Dry yourself off, then come outside to see the world." Such a nice lady.

Duey fell asleep and when he awoke they were
floating along, under the peaceful sky. "How's about
taking a stretch ashore?" Slicker said as she spotted land.
The shore was green and spongy, with lots of trees lining
it. Duey's little eyes searched everywhere for Mama.
Slicker watched, saying nothing. She wrapped herself in a
catalpa leaf, to dry off. Duey found a little nutshell and
made himself a round brown hat, clapping it on between
his winged arms. Duey and Slicker went along a leafy
lane, this queer-shaped lady in her green caftan and her
little friend with his brown round hat.

Soon they passed a carnival. What a sight! Ferris wheels, shooting galleries, popcorn stands, and a snakelike thing that took people up and down hills as they screamed wildly but happily. Dare Slicker and Duey try such a thing? Well, why not?

They waited and waited. Finally a boy came by, reached down, and picked up Slicker, with Duey clinging to her neck. The boy dropped some pennies in the bottle, making a kind of piggy bank out of Slicker. Then he went on the roller coaster, carrying Slicker and Duey along with him. Up they went, and to Duey and Slicker, the people below looked smaller and smaller. A thunderous swish and down they went, hurtling into nothing but thinnest air. They were snatched back, zipped around again. Slicker's caftan billowed up around her as the air rushed by, and, being a lady, she was a bit flustered. Zip, zap went the roller coaster. Duey felt thrilled and sick at the same time. He wanted to hang on to his hat, but it had long ago sailed out. Oh! Forget the hat. If only he could save his head!

When they reached the ground the two friends found their way back to the safety of the forest. Flopping down on the grass, they thanked heaven for the solid earth. After they caught their breath, they headed toward the river, hurrying a bit now that it had grown dark.

They were startled by the sound of a moan, a sad low moan. They looked around and saw a man passing by with a bundle on his back. Another moan. Somehow, it seemed to come from the bundle. Hiding behind a bush, peering into the deep darkness, they watched as one log wiggled and wiggled and finally fell free from the bundle; hitting the ground, it rolled right under the bush.

"Pssst! Pssst!" A hissing sound. "Duey, I'm over here."
Gabby's voice. "It's me, man, I'm hung up. Save me," he
pleaded. And there in the bush Duey found his first
friend—or was he an enemy? Whichever, Duey couldn't
just leave him there. Gabby rolled himself slowly and
painfully from under the bush, bark torn, splinters
showing. "Oh, Duey, buddy boy, help me," he wept.
"Trouble and time have dogged me. What have I done?
What have I done?

The bragging boastful bully was in tears. Take him—
or leave him? What to do? Duey said, "We're going along,
taking things as they come. I don't know if you'd . . .
dig our action." Slicker was amazed to hear Duey sound
so confident—so "hip," if that was the word. It's funny,
she thought, how Duey goes up and down in his moods,
just like the roller coaster, feeling great, feeling low.

"Please! Please!" Gabby peered nervously. "Don't leave me here to die." It was pitiful. "I'll do anything." Slicker came alongside and silently started patching Gabby up, using moist soil from the river's edge to mend his torn bark. Then they made their way, the three now together, to the river, where Duey crept upon Slicker's back and Gabby floated beside them.

Days passed. After a while the current of the river slowed, the river broadened. "What's happening?" asked Duey, who was always the first one to be surprised. Slicker answered, "It was bound to happen, Duey. We're near the ocean now. Most rivers, like our own, run to the sea."

The tide dashed them to and fro. Gabby and Duey nestled against Slicker for dear life. She, too, was afraid, but she did not want to show it, being older. They noticed that the water became dirtier, turned grayer as they went along. Not even Slicker, wise as she was, could guess that the three friends had found their way to a great city, to a huge dock at the water's edge.

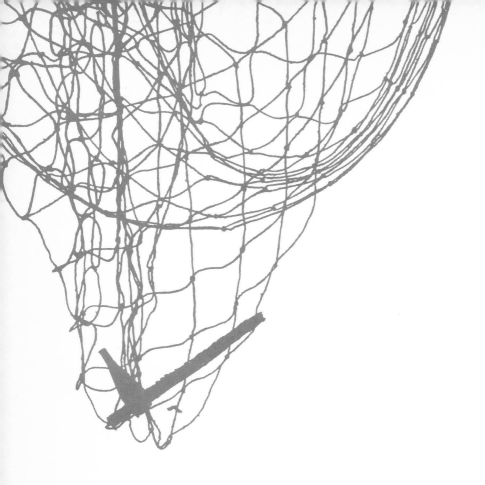

Slicker and Duey and Gabby felt themselves pulled up, out of the water, into the air. They had been caught in the mesh of a cargo net. A ship was unloading, dipping its cargo net over its side to rest on the dock, then back to the ship for another load. Now, caught up as they were, the three friends fell from the strings of the net to the dock. Bump, tinkle, ping. Gabby, Slicker, and Duey fell to the dock. They fell apart—and were separated!

Duey found himself alone—alone for the first time since, well, since he lost Mama. Oh, what a strange and scary feeling it is to be alone. "After all," thought Duey, "the world wouldn't have been made as big as it is if folks were meant to be alone in it." Now, that's a thought, Duey thought, folding his arms over his chest and staying put.

When the sun was up, he stirred himself and found to his amazement that his propellerlike arms caught the air and lifted him off the ground. He could fly with the wind! Off he flew, twirling and swooping along, just the way a maple seedling is supposed to fly before it plants itself for good. Duey spent days and days trying out his wings. He liked touring the city. It was special fun, seeing different sights, and sometimes it was scary, touch and go.

One day he twirled down a broad street, almost catching himself in some wires overhead. He banked, holding his arms stiff, and found himself on a quieter street. Below him were shop doorways and windows, shiny with brass and glass, expensive-looking places. Below him, too, were elegant people strolling down the street. A man passed by, carrying a beautiful carved walking stick.

"Duey! Duey!" The voice was coming from below. Duey looked down, and then he almost crashed with surprise—and joy. It was the stick that was calling him. It was Gabby.

Gabby's Tale

"Duey, you'll never believe it, but listen anyway. Man, am I glad to see you, my old buddy from the road. Man, have we come a long way from home!

"You remember that we got separated. Well, of course you remember. Man, you must have missed me — and probably the old lady, Slicker, missed me, too. I wonder what happened to the old girl? Not a bad old bottle, Slicker, anyway not bad for a bottle. Well, I'll tell you, I was zonked out, just lying there still, when a man picked me up and looked me over real hard. The next thing I knew, the man and I were in a shop, and here's what I heard.

" 'You old fraud,' the man said to the shopkeeper. 'You promised me a cane made of rare hardwood long ago, yet you've come up with exactly nothing. Here, I've brought you a common water-soaked log, since you can't find your own wood.' The man was talking loudly and he was, well, like, sarcastic, you know, and he held me high over his head, like a club.

"The shopkeeper's face had no fear, only a way-out look on it. 'Sir, sir,' he cried, 'in your hand, in your hand. You have in your hand a piece of the rare Puma tree.' Slowly the man lowered me, and weighed me in his hand, and then, smiling, he reached over and shook the hand of the canemaker. 'I knew all along you'd come through for me, old man,' he said. 'I'll be the envy of the town.' With that, he left me with the canemaker.

"Man, oh man, oh man, let me tell you about my operation. All my life people have been saying to me, 'Why don't you make something of yourself?' And now it's happened! The next morning the operation started. The canemaker laid me gently down on a workbench. Swish! The knife cut into me! The pain! Well, pain was never my bag. Yet I held still, no matter what. Then the canemaker rounded my head, tucked in my waist, slimmed me, and shaped a leg.

"When it was all over, the canemaker held me in front of the mirror. I slowly raised my eyes to look at myself. 'It can't be! I was once a pretty cool log, but now I'm a masterpiece.' My head was round as a plum, my body slim as a willow, and I even wore a shoe, tipped in gold.

"If only my family could see me now," Gabby said to Duey, and by now he was tap, tap, tapping down the street, almost out of sight. "Remember me," Gabby cried out, "remember me." And then he was gone. Duey was alone again.

More time had passed than he could remember. One day, flying along like any other day, Duey was swept by the wind down to the docks. Heading for water had become a habit of his, it seemed. As he skimmed by the waterfront, swept close to shore, he paused on a window sill for just a moment. Suddenly he heard a muffled sound. "Duey! Duey!" What a soft voice it was, reminding Duey of other days, like an old song. In the window he saw some brightly colored glass balls. Next to them was a bottle that looked familiar. Was it? Could it be? Yes, it was! It was! It WAS Slicker!

Slicker's Tale

"Duey, my dear, the most extraordinary things have happened. Heavens, I hardly know where to begin. Yes, I do know, but I don't want to remind you of how sad it was for all of us to be parted. When we were dumped so rudely on the dock, so long ago, I was worried sick about you. You are so small and tender and so...well...green.

"I tried to find you, but before I could roll around much, I was picked up by a man with big rough hands. He held me high. Oh, I was certain he was going to smash me on the dock! But he didn't. He just kept looking at me — really right through me, I guess — and then he took me into this shop and put me down on the counter.

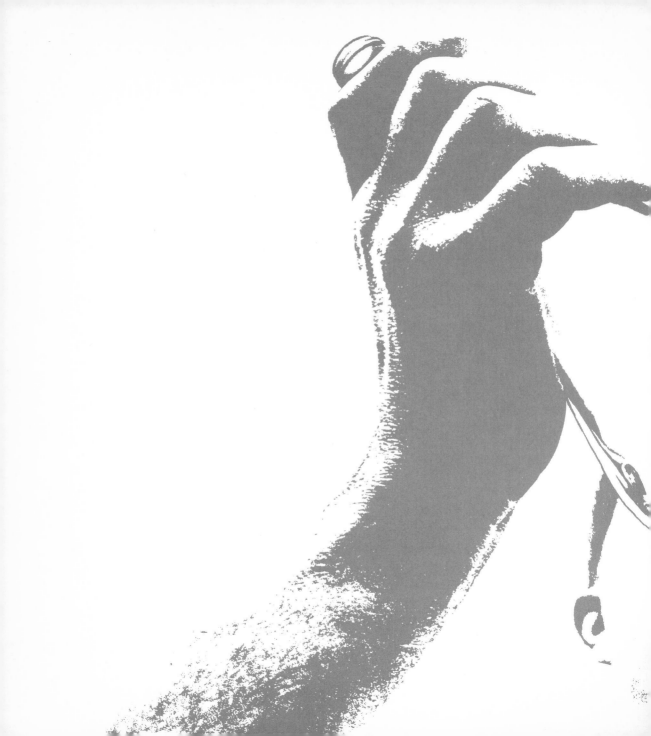

" 'You must be the sailmaker,' he said to the shopkeeper. 'Nobody uses that grand old word much any more,' said the shopkeeper, who was pleased to hear it. 'Yes, I'm a sailmaker, and I've got some sailing and fishing gear in stock. What can I get you?'

" 'Not anything,' said the rough sailor. 'But look. I found this bottle on the wharf. It's a rare piece of glass, this. I'll bet a month's pay that this is Japanese glass, the kind fishermen used to use to float nets in the Sea of Japan. I've seen this blue-green glass there, blue as the sky, green as the sea, unlike any other.'

"Then the sailmaker looked at me closely—I blushed because of all the attention. Really, Duey, I'm just old Slicker, nothing particular about me, you know. I don't make fusses, and I don't fuss over myself. And I don't mean to sound proud.

"The sailor said, 'Keep the bottle, sailmaker. It belongs with fishing gear—nets and boat hooks and bobstays—where it can look at home.' And he left me here.

"Imagine, Duey. I'm a foreigner, probably Japanese. Funny, I don't feel at all foreign. Do I seem foreign to you, Duey? Well, of course I don't. I'm just Slicker, your old friend. But it is nice to think that I was once a fishing float, green and blue, like the sea and sky. I must have been recycled, Duey. So I've been useful to somebody at least twice, once as a float, once as a bottle. And now I'm retired but still useful, I suppose, sitting here. The sailmaker says that I decorate his shop. Isn't that *nice*, Duey?

"Why, Duey, what's wrong?"

Duey sat on the window sill, stunned. "Please, Slicker," he wailed, "why can't we have a few more good times together?"

She waited a long time to answer. Duey's heart slowed. "Sorry, my dear little friend, everyone must find his place, and there is a place for everyone. This is my place, forever. Now, take my word, you will find yours. Being young, you'll probably take longer to find home ground. Being older, I settled down sooner. You have my love forever. Just remember: do the next thing next, Duey."

Duey awoke with a start from a long sleep—how long he did not know. It seemed a long time since he'd seen Slicker, a very long time. He was all alone again. Now he wandered from place to place, drifting, searching. Sometimes he would fly after some gentleman carrying

a handsome gold-tipped cane, and call in an urgent whisper, "Gabby, Gabby." Sometimes he gazed in department-store windows, looking at gorgeous perfume bottles, imagining that he saw Slicker among them. Thinking of his old friends warmed him — and saddened him.

DUEY'S TALE

On a splendid June day, Duey was flying along, thinking about his friends, feeling a little at a loss, when suddenly he felt something else. He had touched down to earth, as he had a lot of times before, but this time it was different.

Touching the earth always felt good — there was always a feeling of belonging. But what was this emotion he now felt? On he moved, faster and faster, pushed along the ground by a swift downdraft, a low wind shoving him along. Once before he had felt like this. Fighting the wind was sapping his energy.

Was he dying? No, that couldn't be it. He felt so strong. Then Duey smiled. After all, he was still a seedling, and seedlings had a whole life ahead of them, didn't they? But just then he stopped moving and came to rest.

Now, each day, each sunrise, he felt more comfortable in his place — more rooted there. He was content — no longer active, it's true, but quite content. He stood still, thinking a lot. Sometimes he wondered whether he would ever amount to anything. Would he be somebody important like Gabby, who came from a rare Puma tree and was now a fine cane with a gold shoe, or Slicker, who surprised everybody, including herself, by turning out to be made of beautiful Japanese fishing glass? But Duey was not envious. He glowed with pride as he remembered his friends.

Duey could not help noticing that he was not only standing still but also growing taller. The grass seemed farther away as he looked down, and one day he was startled to discover that he could see over some bushes, and watch the sun rise over the nearby hillside. What was happening? Had the world gotten smaller? No, Duey thought, the world stays the same: it's how you look at it that changes.

It just happened. Without his really thinking about it,
Duey had grown into a fine young tree. He wore a
smooth bark and had a fine fuzzy head of bright-green
leaves that tossed playfully in the summertime breezes.
He remembered how Mama used to stand high. He was
pleased to be like her, able to cast shade on the weary
traveler, or keep dry the strollers fleeing the sudden
showers.

Duey was happy to grow. He wasn't special or extraordinary, maybe, but he was strong and steady and at peace with the world. One day a boy and girl sat down at his feet and talked and laughed for, oh, the longest time. He heard them call each other playful and loving names, and then speak sadly of how the summer was ending, how each was going far away to school, how long the winter would be before they saw each other again. Then the boy said, "Let's meet here next year, just like this, under this beautiful maple tree." The girl said, "Oh, let's do. Let's meet here. This will be our tree, our very own special tree." The boy and girl walked off, over the hillside and out of sight, as Duey watched.

Duey felt a certain satisfaction come over him. "I'm special!" he said to himself. But how was he special? Was he a rare tree, like the one Gabby came from? Or an exotic foreigner, like Slicker? No. He was just Duey.

But he FELT special, different. Maybe being different was just a matter of having someone's attention. Was Gabby really born of a rare Puma tree? Perhaps not. Perhaps he was just good wood that the canemaker could work with. Was Slicker really any different after the old sailor called her Japanese? She was a nice-looking blue-green bottle even before that. You know, Duey thought, everybody needs to have some attention. That's why people have family and friends.

Duey stood alone, splashing the setting sun's light through his arms. I'm here, he thought. Somebody sees me. I'm Duey, he thought. Somebody knows me.